P9-DNL-098

The Gigantic, Genuine Genie

6

Princess Power

The Gigantic, Genuine Genie

By Suzanne Williams
Illustrated by Chuck Gonzales

HarperTrophy®
An Imprint of HarperCollins*Publishers*

Boca Raton Public Library, Boca Raton, FL

Harper Trophy® is a registered trademark of HarperCollins Publishers.
The Gigantic, Genuine Genie
Text copyright © 2007 by Suzanne Williams
Illustrations copyright © 2007 by Chuck Gonzales
All rights reserved. Printed in the United States of America.
No part of this book may be used or reproduced in any
manner whatsoever without written permission except in
the case of brief quotations embodied in critical articles and
reviews. For information address HarperCollins Children's
Books, a division of HarperCollins Publishers, 1350 Avenue
of the Americas, New York, NY 10019.

www.harpercollinschildrens.com

Library of Congress Cataloging-in-Publication Data
Williams, Suzanne, 1949–
  The gigantic, genuine genie / by Suzanne Williams ; illustrated
by Chuck Gonzales.—1st HarperTrophy ed.
    p.   cm.—(Princess power ; 6)
  Summary: At the bazaar, Princess Fatima buys a beautiful bottle that holds a tiny, powerless genie, who proves that there are
many advantages to being small, and that being helpful and brave
does not require magic.
  ISBN-10: 0-06-078308-7 (pbk. bdg.)—ISBN-13: 978-0-06-078308-2
(pbk. bdg.)
  [1. Princesses—Fiction. 2. Genies—Fiction. 3. Friendship—Fiction.
4. Magic—Fiction. 5. Adventure and adventurers—Fiction.] I.
Gonzales, Chuck, ill. II. Title.
PZ7.W66824Gi 2007   2006028655
[Fic]—dc22   CIP
                                                    AC

Typography by Jennifer Heuer
❖
First Harper Trophy edition, 2007

To Gene and Ginny Williams,
my terrific "in-laws"

Contents

1 At the Bazaar — 1

2 The Ruby Bottle — 11

3 Wishes — 19

4 Jasper's Story — 27

5 The Grand Genie — 37

6 Shooting Stars — 46

7 The Runaway Carpet — 52

8 Back to the Palace — 61

9 The Thieves — 71

10 Locked Up — 82

11 To the Rescue — 93

12 Celebration — 101

The Gigantic, Genuine Genie

At the Bazaar

Princess Fatima was practicing loop-the-loops on her flying carpet when she spotted three carriages. They were climbing up the long, tree-lined drive to her parents' palace. Giving a whoop, she dove toward the ground, pulling up at the last second to land neatly beside the front gardens. No sooner had she landed than the carriages clattered to a stop. Fatima's friends—the princesses Lysandra,

Tansy, and Elena—flung open the doors and leaped out.

"Welcome!" said Fatima, hugging them each in turn. "I'm so glad you could come."

Tansy stared at the black marble palace in front of her. "Wow!" she exclaimed. "This place is *huge*."

Fatima smiled. The castle Tansy and her six brothers lived in was small, but it had seemed cozy to Fatima.

In a few minutes, servants arrived to carry the princesses' bags into the palace. "I know you just got here," said Fatima, "but I wonder if you'd like to fly into town and shop at the bazaar. It closes in a couple of hours. If you want to see it, we should go there first thing."

Lysandra brushed back her blond waves. "I'd love to see it. There's something I'd like to look for."

"Sounds good to me," said Tansy.

"Me, too," Elena agreed.

Fatima grinned. "Then let's go!"

The princesses settled onto the flying carpet. Fatima pulled up on the front edge, and the carpet rose into the air.

"Whee!" said Lysandra. "I just *love* flying."

The girls followed the tree-lined drive until they came to a river that flowed past small, flat-roofed houses. In the distance the striped tents of the bazaar billowed up like sheets flapping on a clothesline.

"Wow!" said Tansy. "I can't wait to see what's under those tents."

Fatima landed the carpet just outside the bazaar. The princesses scrambled off, and Fatima rolled up the carpet and strapped it onto her back. "This way," she said, leading them under the tents.

The girls joined the throng of people winding their way past displays of beautiful copper trays, leather bags, woven tablecloths, and decorated pots. The shouts of merchants hawking their wares blended with bawling camels and chattering monkeys atop their master's shoulders.

The princesses stopped to look at some necklaces. A silver-and-turquoise one caught Fatima's eye. She tried it on. "Pretty," she said, admiring herself in a mirror. "What do you think, Lysandra?"

But Lysandra didn't reply.

Fatima looked around but couldn't see her anywhere. Panicking, she called to Tansy and Elena, who were also trying on necklaces. "Quick! Lysandra must have wandered away. We've got to find her before she gets lost!"

The three princesses ran through the bazaar calling Lysandra's name over and over again. They finally found her at a table piled high with woven rugs.

"You shouldn't wander off like that!" Fatima scolded. "I was worried about you!"

"We all were," said Tansy.

"We were afraid you'd gotten lost!" Elena said.

"Sorry," Lysandra apologized. "I saw these rugs and I . . . well, I've always wanted a carpet like yours, Fatima." She ran a hand over the rug. It was brightly colored, with red and yellow flowers on an emerald background. "Isn't it beautiful? And it's only twenty gold coins. Can you believe it?"

Tansy held up the carpet. "It's gorgeous!"

The rug merchant nodded. "A very nice carpet. Top quality and a good price."

"I'm going to buy it." Lysandra pulled her magic purse from around her neck, shook out a handful of coins, and began to count them.

"Twenty gold coins *is* a good price," Fatima said, "for a carpet you can *walk* on."

Lysandra frowned. "You mean these carpets can't fly?"

The merchant's eyebrows shot up. "A *flying* carpet?" he said. "My dear, I am so sorry. Flying carpets are very rare and very expensive."

"And unlikely to be found in a bazaar," added Fatima.

Rubbing the back of his neck, the merchant said, "This is true." He looked at Lysandra. "I'm sorry, but I cannot help you."

As they left the merchant's stall, Fatima said, "Forget about finding a flying carpet, Lysandra. There just aren't that many around."

Lysandra frowned. "If I didn't know better,

Fatima, I'd think you didn't *want* me to have one."

"Nonsense," said Fatima. But a tiny part of her wondered if Lysandra was right. As the princesses continued through the bazaar, Fatima shrugged the thought away.

In a far corner they came upon a pot-bellied old man selling colored glass bottles with stoppered tops.

"Aren't they pretty?" said Elena.

Fatima nodded. She picked up a ruby bottle that she thought would look nice on her dresser. "How much is this one?" she asked the merchant.

He grinned. "You have a good eye," he said. "That one is the most precious. It holds a gigantic, genuine genie."

Fatima rolled her eyes. "A genie, indeed! How much?" she asked again.

"Ten gold coins."

"Bats and bullfrogs!" Fatima exclaimed. "Even if there really were a genie inside, I still wouldn't pay that much." But she liked the bottle, which was shaped like a gourd with a long, thin neck. "I'll pay *three* coins."

"*Seven,*" said the old man. "You think I'd let this genie go for such a cheap price?"

"*Four,*" said Fatima. "If there really were a

genie inside, you'd keep the bottle yourself."

"*Six*," said the old man. "What do I need with a genie? I'm too old for wishes."

"*Five*," said Fatima. "But only because I like the bottle."

"*Sold!*" cried the old man.

Fatima paid him the five coins. He wound a soft cloth around the bottle, carefully placed the bottle in a bag, and handed it to Fatima.

"May the genie do you much good!" he called after her as the princesses walked away.

"Yeah, right," Fatima muttered under her breath. What a crazy old man!

The Ruby Bottle

FATIMA HELD ON TO THE BAG TIGHTLY. SHE AND her friends left the old man's stall and rejoined the stream of people wandering through the bazaar.

"Let's unwrap the bottle and open it right now," said Tansy.

"Yes, let's!" Lysandra agreed.

Fatima stared at her friends. "You don't really think there's a genie inside, do you?"

Elena looked wistful. "But wouldn't it be wonderful if it were true?"

"Maybe," said Fatima. She didn't want to admit it, but deep down she hoped that the old man had actually been telling the truth. "I'll open the bottle when we get back to the palace. I don't want to unwrap it here, where it's so crowded. If somebody bumped me, the bottle could break."

After looking at a few more stalls, the princesses left the bazaar. When they were outside the tents, Fatima unrolled her carpet.

"I can fly us back if you'd like," Lysandra offered. "Then you can hold on to your bottle to make sure it doesn't roll off the carpet."

Fatima hesitated. "All right," she said. Lysandra had flown her carpet several times before and was pretty good at it. With practice, she could learn to fly as well as Fatima—maybe even better. Fatima's stomach sank at the thought. She *liked* being the best at flying. "Pull back sharply," Fatima directed as they lifted off. But she didn't need to say anything; Lysandra's takeoffs and landings were nearly perfect.

The return trip didn't take long. With only a mild jolt, Lysandra set the carpet down in front of the palace. "Good job," Fatima said briskly. She rolled up the carpet and strapped it onto her back. Then the four princesses trooped inside.

Fatima's parents, King Mustafa and Queen Saruca, greeted the girls. Like Fatima, they both had dark hair and skin, and almond-shaped eyes that sparkled with energy. Fatima thought her father's long beard and flowing robes gave him an especially regal appearance. And her mother was strikingly beautiful—tall and slender, with an oval face and high, delicate cheekbones.

They chatted a bit until King Mustafa was

called away on royal business. Queen Saruca also excused herself. "I must dash off to a meeting of the Royal Ladies Arts Society," she explained, "but I'll look forward to talking with you girls at dinner tonight."

"Come on," Fatima said to her friends. "I'll show you the palace."

The princesses followed Fatima through rooms lavishly decorated with paintings of peacocks and elephants, misty mountains, and

dusty caravans. "I've never seen so much art-work in one place before, except in a museum," commented Elena. She paused to admire an orchard landscape.

"My parents collect art from all over the world," said Fatima. "It's kind of their hobby."

Lysandra whistled. "These paintings must be worth a fortune!"

"My brother Jonah would die to be able to paint like this," Tansy said.

Leaving the paintings behind, the princesses entered an elegant courtyard. A tiered fountain stood in a pool of water, surrounded by a wide strip of lawn, sweet-smelling flowers, and a tree loaded with heavy, ripe oranges.

"Mmm," said Lysandra. "Those oranges look delicious."

Fatima led her friends from the courtyard straight into her bedroom suite. It was so large, it had space for a sofa, chairs, and a huge wardrobe. The servants had delivered the princesses' bags to the door, and a second double bed had been brought in to accommodate the guests.

"Your room is so beautiful," Elena said, looking around in awe.

Tansy flopped onto the extra bed. "And comfy," she declared.

Leaving the doors to the suite open, Fatima stepped back into the courtyard. "Shall we open the bottle now?" she asked.

"Yes, yes, yes!" the princesses chorused.

Fatima crossed the lawn and sat down near the fountain. Her friends gathered around her. Unstrapping her carpet, Fatima let it fall to the ground. Then she drew the bottle out of its bag and unwound the cloth.

"Here goes nothing," she muttered, holding the ruby bottle in front of her. She pulled out the glass stopper.

And *nothing* is exactly what happened.

Fatima shrugged, feeling foolish for having entertained even a glimmer of hope. Making a joke of it, she turned the bottle upside down and smacked it on the bottom. "Come out, come out, gigantic genie!" she called. And, to everyone's surprise, out plopped a quivering, pink, pear-shaped creature—no bigger than a caterpillar!

The creature landed on Fatima's knee and

waved two tiny arms as it teetered on two tiny feet. Finally, catching its balance, it straightened up.

The princesses stared at the pear-shaped creature. Fatima could just make out a tuft of yellow hair on top of its tiny head. "Are you a . . . a *genie*?" she asked.

"As angels sing, I'm the genuine thing," the genie said with a tiny bow. "Now stand up and cheer because Jasper is here!"

Wishes

"HE'S HARDLY GIGANTIC, IS HE?" TANSY whispered in Fatima's ear.

"No kidding," Fatima whispered back.

Lysandra squinted at Jasper. "Can you grant wishes?"

The genie hopped up and down. "Is a whale a fish? Just tell me your wish."

"Actually, a whale *isn't* a fish," Tansy said with a smile. "It's a mammal."

Fatima grinned. "True."

Elena nudged Fatima. "Since you bought the bottle, the wishes should be yours."

Her friends nodded in agreement.

"But I don't know what to wish for," Fatima protested.

Jasper rubbed his hands together. "Don't be shy. I'm here to satisfy. Be my guest. Wish for the best."

Fatima winced. "I wish you wouldn't speak in bad rhyme."

The genie waved a hand. "Granted."

"Wait a second," said Fatima. "That didn't require any magic."

"Of course it did," said Jasper. "You think it's easy for me not to speak in rhyme?"

"Just because something is difficult doesn't mean it takes magic to do it," argued Fatima. "But never mind. We'll try another wish.

Does anyone have an idea?"

Lysandra's stomach growled. Glancing up at the orange tree, she said, "I wish I had an orange this very instant."

"Is that it?" scoffed Jasper. "You're certainly easy to please."

"Well, what's wrong with that?" Lysandra shrugged. "I'm hungry."

"All right then. Listen up, everyone," said the genie. "Cover your eyes for a big surprise."

"You just rhymed again," Fatima said with a giggle. But, like the other three princesses, she dutifully put her hands over her eyes.

After what seemed like several minutes, Fatima heard the rustling of a tree branch and the sound of oranges falling to the ground. Peeking through her fingers, she spied Jasper sliding down the tree. Then he heaved himself against one of the fallen

oranges until it started to roll. It came to a
stop at Lysandra's feet.

"You can open your eyes now," he said,
panting heavily.

"Well, will you look at that!" exclaimed

Lysandra. She winked at the others as she
began to peel the orange. Fatima suspected
they'd all heard the tree shake and the oranges
fall.

The genie puffed himself up as best he

could—maybe another eighth of an inch. Pumping his fist in the air, he chanted, "I'm the best in the east and the . . ." He paused, glancing at Fatima. "North," he finished.

Fatima arched an eyebrow. Now she could see why the merchant had been willing to part with the genie so cheaply. "I wish you'd go back in your bottle," she said only half jokingly.

Jasper looked surprised, and then hurt. He might have even slumped a little, though it was difficult to tell since he was so small. "Well, if that's what you want," he said. "Your wish is my command . . . unless, of course, you'd like to change your mind."

Laying a gentle hand on Fatima's shoulder, Elena said, "I don't think Jasper wants to go back in his bottle just yet."

Fatima crossed her arms stubbornly. That

genie was beginning to get on her nerves. "Too bad. I bought him. He's mine now, and he has to do what I say." Even to her own ears, her words sounded mean, but Fatima didn't know how to take them back.

She held out the ruby bottle and Jasper climbed onto it. He inched his way toward the top, taking forever to get there. "Can't you just turn into a vapor and let the bottle suck you in?" Fatima asked impatiently.

Jasper grunted. "That's the easy way. I do it differently." At last he reached the mouth of the bottle. Plopping his legs inside, he struggled to push his bottom past the bottle's neck. But it was no good. "Help!" he cried. "I'm stuck!"

Fatima turned the bottle upside down and gave it a smack. The genie plopped headfirst into her lap. Fatima helped him to stand upright. "You *can't* vaporize, can you?"

"No, I can't," Jasper admitted with a snif-fle. A tiny tear rolled down his cheek. "The truth is, I've lost all my powers. I'm completely useless."

Jasper's Story

NOW THAT JASPER HAD ADMITTED THE TRUTH, Fatima felt sorry for him. "Please tell us your story," she begged. "How did you lose your powers?"

The princesses all leaned forward, eager to hear his response.

Jasper sighed and settled himself on Fatima's knee again. "You'll probably find this hard to believe, but once upon a time I was a very big and powerful genie—not this teensy weensy thing you see now."

"Being small isn't so bad," said Tansy. She was the shortest of the four princesses.

"It wasn't my physical size that got me into trouble so much as the size of my ego," he said. "I used to laugh at the puny powers of others. Take Cinderella's fairy godmother, for instance. She could only grant wishes that lasted till midnight. 'How pathetic is that?' I used to say." He hung his head. "Now *I'm* the one who's pathetic."

"You poor thing," said Elena. "But what happened to make you lose your powers?"

Jasper blushed. "One day I got a little too boastful. I challenged the Grand Genie to a wish-granting contest."

"The *Grand* Genie?" repeated Lysandra. "Is that like a king or queen?"

Jasper nodded. "I didn't know it was the

Grand Genie, though."

"Why not?" asked Fatima.

"The Grand Genie was disguised as a wizard. You know, with a long, white beard, a robe with stars, and a tall, pointy hat. Anyway, we found a young woman in need of help and took turns granting her wishes. I kept showing off. When the woman wished for money to help her sick mother, the wizard—that is, the Grand Genie—gave her just the number of gold coins she said she needed. No more, no less.

"Ha, I thought. What a stingy miser you are. And I showered the woman with buckets of rubies, diamonds, and emeralds."

"Was she grateful?" Elena asked.

"I'm not sure," Jasper said. "She seemed like such a sweet young woman when we picked her out for our contest, but when she saw all those jewels, a funny glint came into

her eyes. She began to demand grander and grander things: fancy dresses, a carriage, a castle. She even wanted to become queen."

"Hmm," said Lysandra. "Sounds like she got carried away with her wishes."

"It was my own fault," said Jasper. "I shouldn't have given her so many jewels in

the first place. Anyway, the wizard kept trying
to convince the young woman to wish for
simpler things. 'Would a hundred fancy
dresses *really* make you happy?' the wizard
asked her. 'How about just one or two, for
special occasions?'

'What's the matter?' I asked. 'Afraid you'll

get worn out making all those dresses?' And then I said something even worse. . . ." Jasper's voice trailed off. He was clearly embarrassed.

"What was that?" prompted Fatima.

"I called the Grand Genie a *girl*. I said, 'I bet you're not a real wizard at all. Only a girl could have such weak powers.'"

"Humph," said Lysandra. "In case you hadn't noticed, *we're* girls—princesses, in fact. That was an awful thing to say."

"And anyway, it's not true," said Tansy.

"That's right," said Fatima. "Girls can be just as strong and brave as boys."

"And often smarter," added Elena.

Jasper nodded. "So I found out. The wizard got mad at me and roared, 'I've never been so insulted in my life!' Then she whipped off her beard."

"*She?*" said Fatima. "You mean the Grand

Genie was . . ."

". . . a girl." finished Jasper. "Well, *female*, anyway."

The princesses couldn't help smiling.

"What happened next?" asked Elena.

"First she sent the young woman away with a handful of coins and two new dresses. Then she turned to me. 'I was testing you today,' she said. 'And, unfortunately, you failed. Genies who use their powers unwisely don't deserve to have them. Granting wishes above a human's true need encourages greed and only creates unhappiness in the end.'"

"Wow," said Tansy. "Those are strong words."

"Greed does make people unhappy," Elena said.

"So then the Grand Genie stripped you of your powers?" asked Fatima.

Jasper nodded sadly.

"Can't you earn them back?" Lysandra asked.

The genie sighed. "I don't know how. I'm afraid my powers are gone for good."

"I think that's unfair," said Tansy.

"You do?" Jasper asked.

Tansy nodded. "Everyone makes mistakes. We all deserve second chances."

"I wonder what would happen if we *wished* your powers back," said Elena.

"Won't work," replied Jasper. "My last master—the merchant who sold me—tried it already." He shrugged. "Let's face it. I'm worthless."

"Wait a second," said Fatima. "Maybe the princess cure would work." She winked at her friends.

"You mean the cure that changes enchanted frogs back into princes?" asked Lysandra.

"And transforms enchanted apples, too?" asked Tansy.

"The very one," said Fatima.

Elena smiled. "We could try it."

"What are you going to do?" Jasper asked nervously.

"Relax," said Fatima. "One of us is going to kiss you, that's all."

"*Kiss* me?" Jasper blushed again. Even his tuft of yellow hair blazed scarlet. "Genies don't like to be kissed."

Tansy snorted. "Believe me. This won't be any fun for us, either. But if there's a chance it might help you regain your powers . . ."

"All right," Jasper interrupted. "But I don't want to watch."

Fatima shrugged. "Fine. Close your eyes then."

"Who's going to do it?" asked Tansy.

"Not me," said Lysandra.

"Me neither," said Fatima. "And I don't care if I am the oldest. It's someone else's turn this time."

"I'll do it," Elena volunteered. "After all, I'm the next oldest." She reached out her hand and Jasper timidly climbed onto it. Then Elena lifted him up to her lips. As she carried him closer, he squeezed his eyes shut. Elena puckered her lips and gave him a big smack.

The Grand Genie

The force of Elena's kiss knocked Jasper backward. He tumbled off her hand, but Fatima caught him in midair. "Well, your size hasn't changed," she said, squinting at him. "But your powers may have returned. Shall we try another wish?"

"Okay," said Jasper, looking a bit doubtful.

"I have one," Lysandra volunteered, "if you don't mind that I already made a wish."

"*I* can't think of anything," said Tansy.

"Me, neither," said Elena.

"Then go for it," said Fatima.

Lysandra gave her a sideways glance. "I wish I had a flying carpet," she said.

Fatima pursed her lips. She hated to admit it, but Lysandra had been right; she *didn't* want her friend to have a flying carpet. If Lysandra had one too, then Fatima's carpet wouldn't be as special. And neither, thought Fatima, would she.

Concentrating intensely, Jasper squeezed his eyes shut. He pressed his tiny hands to his forehead. "Granted!" he said at last. His eyes popped open, and he looked around. "I did it!" he squealed.

For a brief second, Fatima's heart leaped into her throat. But then she saw that Jasper was pointing to the carpet at her feet. "That's *my* flying carpet," she said, trying not to sound too relieved that Lysandra's wish hadn't come true.

"Oh," the genie said glumly.

Lysandra looked disappointed too.

"Cheer up, Jasper," said Elena. "We'll find another way to help you regain your powers."

"Didn't the Grand Genie leave you with *any* hope that you could get your powers back someday?" asked Tansy.

Jasper thought for a moment. "She did say *one* thing," he said slowly. "I was so upset at the time, I'm not sure I remember it clearly. But I think she said, 'Your powers will return on the day everyone acknowledges you no longer need them.'"

"How strange," said Lysandra. "I suppose you would no longer need your powers if you were . . ." Her voice trailed off.

". . . dead?" Fatima finished for her. She frowned. "But genies don't die, do they?"

"That reminds me of a joke," Jasper said, brightening a little. "Old genies never die. They just evaporate."

"Huh?" asked Tansy.

"*Evaporate*," Jasper repeated. "You know—when a vapor disappears. Genies are always vaporizing to get in and out of bottles and lamps. I used to be able to do it too."

"Oh," said Tansy. "I get it." The princesses

smiled, but no one laughed.

Jasper sighed. "I guess it's not a very good joke."

"It's better than his rhymes," Lysandra whispered to Fatima.

"Back to the Grand Genie," said Elena. "I wonder if 'the day you no longer need them' means the day you can do *without* your powers."

Jasper stared at her. "What? I don't get it."

Elena tried to explain. "Even without magic, you can still help others. Maybe your powers will return when you quit trying to use magic."

"But how can I help without magic?" Jasper looked puzzled.

"Bats and bullfrogs!" Fatima exclaimed. "You've been doing that all along! You didn't use magic to get Lysandra an orange; you only *pretended* to."

"That's right!" said Lysandra. "And that was a very helpful thing to do. The orange was delicious."

"I'm glad you liked it," said Jasper. "So you think if I gave up pretending, and did helpful things without trying to use magic, my powers might come back?"

"Maybe," said Elena. "It's worth a try."

Tansy nodded.

"All right," said Jasper. "So what should I do?"

Fatima shrugged. "You could help out around the palace."

"How?" he asked.

Fatima thought for a moment. Jasper was so small that most things would be hard for him to do. Of course, for some tasks, his size would be an advantage. "I know!" she exclaimed. "Last week I lost a pearl earring. It must be in my room—or out here in the courtyard somewhere—but I haven't been able to find it. Maybe you could look for it."

Jasper jumped up and down. "Easy peasey!" he said. "When things need to be found, you'll be glad I'm around. I'll start near the ground."

"You're speaking in rhyme again," Fatima said, rolling her eyes.

"Sorry," said Jasper. He slid down her leg

and hopped off. In a moment, the princesses saw his head bobbing up and down in the lawn.

Tansy grinned. "That'll keep him busy for a while."

"I should think so," said Elena.

Fatima stood up. "It's about time for dinner. My parents will be expecting us in the Banquet Hall. Shall we go now?"

Her friends nodded. "I'm famished," said Tansy.

Fatima told Jasper they were going to dinner and would return in an hour. "Would you like us to bring something back for you?" she asked.

"No, thanks," he said. "You go dine. I'll be fine."

Fatima ignored the rhyme, but Elena called back, "See you later, alligator!" Afterward, she whispered to her friends, "Do you think it's okay to leave him alone?"

"Are you worried that he might get lost?" asked Tansy. "Jasper *is* awfully small."

"It's not that," said Elena. "It's just that he seems to get these big ideas about what he can do."

"Jasper will be fine," said Lysandra. "In fact, he'll probably *still* be looking for Fatima's earring when we get back from dinner."

Fatima nodded in agreement. After all, how much trouble could one tiny, powerless genie cause in only an hour?

Shooting Stars

THE PRINCESSES JOINED KING MUSTAFA AND Queen Saruca at a shiny mahogany table that stretched nearly the entire length of the Banquet Hall. Once the princesses were seated, servants brought in several dishes, including partridge, fish, lamb, rice, bread, and vegetables.

Queen Saruca smiled at the princesses.

"Did you have a pleasant afternoon?"

"Oh, yes!" Tansy and Elena exclaimed.

Lysandra grinned. "We bought a stunning bottle at the bazaar and there was a . . . ouch!"

Fatima kicked her under the table. She wasn't sure why, but she didn't want her parents to know about Jasper. Not yet, anyway.

King Mustafa looked up from the head of the table. "Is something the matter?" he asked.

"It's nothing," Lysandra mumbled, giving Fatima a hurt look. "I accidentally bit my tongue, that's all."

Queen Saruca leaned forward in her chair. "You were saying something about a bottle," she prompted Lysandra.

Lysandra reached down to rub her shin. "Yes, well, Fatima can tell you about it."

Fatima smiled at her mother. "There's nothing to tell, really. It's a pretty bottle—a bright ruby color. I thought it might look nice on my dresser."

"You'll have to show it to me sometime," said Queen Saruca. She loved beautiful

objects almost as much as beautiful paintings.

"I will," Fatima said.

When dinner was over, a troupe of acrobats entertained everyone with juggling acts and tumbling tricks. During the show, Fatima glanced out the window. The sun had begun

to set and she was thinking her friends might like to go for an evening ride.

But she gasped at what she saw outside.

"What's wrong?" asked Elena.

Fatima pointed to the sky.

Elena looked out the window just in time to see a colorful streak sweep by. It was moving almost as fast as a shooting star. "That couldn't be . . ."

"I hope not," Fatima interrupted. "But it sure looked like it. And someone must be on board because it doesn't fly itself." She hurriedly excused herself from the table and signaled for the other princesses to follow. As they raced back to Fatima's quarters, Elena explained to Tansy and Lysandra what they thought they'd seen in the sky.

In the courtyard, the girls checked around the fountain for the flying carpet. Just as

Fatima had feared, it was gone.

"Jasper!" the princesses called, over and over again. But he was missing, too.

The Runaway Carpet

ELENA'S EYES GREW ROUND. "YOU DON'T THINK someone has stolen the carpet and kidnapped Jasper, do you?"

Fatima shook her head. "I couldn't see anyone on the carpet. It seemed to be flying itself. But Jasper's so small, I wouldn't be able to see him. The only explanation I can think of is that Jasper decided to go for a ride."

"But he's much too small to control a flying carpet," Lysandra said. "He'll never be able to land it without help."

"I know." Fatima pressed her lips together in a tight line.

"Is there anything we can do?" asked Elena.

Fatima frowned. "We'll have to try to find him and coach him back down. But he could be miles away by now."

"Do you have horses?" asked Lysandra. "We could cover more ground on horseback than on foot."

"Yes," said Fatima, "but I haven't ridden in years. I haven't needed to, with a flying carpet."

"That's okay," said Lysandra. "We can double up. I'm great with horses."

"I know how to ride too," said Tansy.

"Elena can come with me."

Fatima tucked Jasper's empty bottle under her belt as the princesses ran to the stables. They saddled up two horses and galloped in the direction where they'd last seen the carpet. After a few miles the girls finally caught sight of it, hovering above some scrubby-looking trees and bushes at the edge of a field.

The princesses raced over to the trees. Fatima cupped her hands around her mouth. "Jasper!" she called out. "Are you up there?"

"Yes!" The cry was so faint, they could barely hear it. After a pause, he added, "Please help me. I'm scared!"

As much as Fatima wanted to scold Jasper for taking her carpet, she realized that the

most important thing now was to get him—and her carpet—safely down to the ground. "Listen up!" she said to him. "Crawl to the front of the carpet and pull down the edge."

"I can't," he said, sniffling. "I'll fall off."

"Not if you're careful," said Fatima. "Just take it slow and easy."

"All right," Jasper whimpered. "I'll try."

The princesses held their breaths as they waited, while the horses impatiently stamped the ground.

After several minutes had passed with no word from Jasper, Fatima shouted, "Have you reached the edge yet?"

"Almost," Jasper replied. His voice sounded shaky. Another minute went by. Suddenly the genie gave a cry, and the carpet plummeted past the trees, landing in a prickly bush.

The girls slid off their horses and ran toward him. Elena peered into the bush. "Jasper!" she shouted. "Where are you? Are you okay?"

"Here I am." Jasper crawled out from underneath some leaves.

Elena reached out to him and he hopped onto her palm. She looked him over carefully. "You've got a bad scratch on your arm," she said. Taking a small blue bottle from the pocket of her gown, she uncapped it and poured a drop of the creamy, white lotion onto her fingertip. Then she rubbed the lotion over Jasper's tiny arm. The scratch disappeared instantly.

Jasper smiled. "Now *that's* magic!"

"Yes, a subject you know next to nothing about," Fatima said with a scowl. She was holding her mangled carpet, which was covered with prickles. "Just look at my carpet. It's ruined!"

"I'm sorry," said Jasper, dropping his head.

"Sorry's not good enough," Fatima snapped. "It'll take hours to pull out these prickles. And look at all the torn threads!" Lysandra put an arm around Fatima's shoulders to calm her, but Fatima shrugged her off. Even though she knew she was being harsh, she couldn't seem to stop herself. "Why did you take my carpet?" she demanded.

"I didn't mean to," Jasper whined. "I was only going to use it to help me look for your earring in the courtyard. I thought I could make it skim just an inch or two above the ground."

Fatima frowned. "I should've known better than to leave you alone. You obviously can't be trusted."

"Hold on," said Tansy. "I'm sure Jasper didn't mean any harm."

Fatima picked a prickle out of her carpet. "Maybe not, but he's caused more than enough trouble for one day." She slipped the ruby bottle from under her belt and pulled out the stopper.

Jasper stared at the bottle in horror. "*Please* don't make me go back in there. I'll be good. I promise!"

Fatima hesitated for a moment. But then in a stern voice, she declared, "Jasper, I order you to return to your bottle!"

"All right," Jasper said with a sigh. "If that's what you really want." With his shoulders slumped, he walked toward Fatima. She tipped the bottle sideways and rested it on the ground. He tried to squeeze in headfirst, but got stuck again, so Fatima gave his bottom a little shove. "Oomph!" squealed Jasper, and he shot the rest of the way inside.

Avoiding the shocked looks on her friends' faces, Fatima stoppered the bottle. "That should keep him from making any more mischief tonight," she said grimly. But deep down she wondered if she was doing the right thing.

Back to the Palace

FATIMA SET THE BOTTLE ON THE GROUND WHILE she rolled up her carpet and strapped it onto her back. She'd have to finish picking out the prickles later. And she'd have to find a weaver to rework or replace the broken threads. Fatima sighed. What a lot of trouble Jasper had turned out to be!

All the way home, the princesses were silent. When they reached the palace, they went straight to Fatima's quarters. Fatima unstrapped her carpet and let it drop to the floor. Then she set Jasper's bottle on her dresser. "I'm going to say good night to my parents," Fatima told her friends. "Do you just want to wait for me here?" The three princesses nodded.

King Mustafa and Queen Saruca looked up from their books and smiled at Fatima when she entered their room. She wanted to tell them about Jasper and everything that had happened, but they looked so relaxed that she decided to wait until morning. Instead, she kissed them good night and walked back to her quarters.

As she neared the courtyard, Fatima heard her friends talking. "I feel sorry for Jasper," Lysandra was saying. "Fatima's so hard on him."

Fatima gulped, wondering if they all felt

that way. She paused in the hall outside the courtyard to hear what the others would say.

"I suppose she's disappointed that Jasper doesn't have any powers," said Elena.

"But *he* can't help that," said Tansy. "I wish she was nicer to him."

Nicer to Jasper? After what he'd done to her carpet? Fatima frowned. Why shouldn't Jasper spend some time alone in his bottle? It wasn't exactly a punishment. The bottle was his home, after all—even if he had been reluctant to go back inside. Anyway, he'd be safer there. Jasper was so small that someone could accidentally step on him if he was left to wander around by himself. Really, it was for his own good.

Fatima continued into the courtyard. Tansy was sitting cross-legged on the edge of the pool, polishing her wooden flute. It was a magical flute, and whenever Tansy played it,

everyone's thoughts could be heard aloud.
"Are you going to play for us?" Fatima asked.

Tansy yawned. "I thought I would, but I've
changed my mind. I'm really tired." She got
up and put her flute away.

The girls were already wearing their

nightgowns. "I'm ready to go to sleep," said Elena.

"So am I," said Lysandra.

"I guess I'm pretty tired, too," said Fatima. "It's been a long day, after all." She followed the princesses into her room and changed into her nightgown. Then she sat down at her dresser to brush out her long, dark hair. Beside her brush stood the ruby bottle. She hoped Jasper was okay in there.

The princesses hugged each other good night and climbed into bed. But even though she was tired, Fatima was unable to sleep. She couldn't stop thinking about Jasper. Maybe her friends were right; maybe she *had* been too hard on him.

Finally, Fatima lit a candle and slid out of bed. Careful not to wake the others, she tiptoed to her dresser and pulled the stopper out of Jasper's bottle. She tried to see inside, but it was too dark. "Jasper," she whispered. "Are you awake?"

"Who wants to know?" a sulky voice replied.

Fatima pursed her lips. "It's me. Fatima."

From the depths of the bottle, Jasper sighed. "I can't grant you a wish, you know— even if you are my master."

"I know," said Fatima. "That's not why I want to talk to you. I don't even *want* to be your master."

There was a pause. "You don't?"

"No, not really." Fatima wondered if she would have felt the same way if Jasper *did* have powers. Yes, she thought, because it wasn't right to be someone's master. Besides, being Jasper's master had only made her cross with him. Jasper needed to learn to take charge of his own life. Fatima took a deep breath. "I'm letting you go."

"You mean I can leave the bottle?" asked Jasper.

"Yes." Fatima tipped the bottle onto its side. The genie crawled out headfirst, and

Fatima pulled gently on his hands so that he didn't get stuck.

"Thanks," said Jasper after he was standing on the dresser. He looked around the room. "So it's okay if I choose a new place to sleep?"

Fatima smiled. "You don't understand. I'm letting you go, forever. You're *free*. You can be your own master now."

Jasper stared at her. "But I don't know how to be free. I've always had a master."

"You'll get the hang of it," Fatima said. "But you can stay here for the night, if you'd like."

"Where else would I go?" asked Jasper.

Fatima spread her arms wide. "Anywhere you want. The world's a big place and there's a lot to see. From now on, you get to make your *own* decisions." She paused. "But I'd appreciate it if you left my flying carpet alone."

"Don't worry." Jasper shuddered. "There's no way I'm getting back on *that* thing again."

"Good." Fatima smiled. "Now, where would you like to spend the night?"

Jasper looked around the room, then into the courtyard. "Could I sleep at the top of the fountain? I like high places—as long as they don't move."

"Sure," said Fatima. The fountain had been turned off for the night. Jasper would be safe there, as long as he didn't fall into the pool. "Do you know how to swim?" she asked.

"Like a fish," said Jasper. Fatima hoped it wasn't another one of his boasts.

Jasper climbed onto her hand and she carried him into the courtyard. With her free hand holding the hem of her nightgown, Fatima waded into the pool and stretched up to reach the top of the fountain. Jasper hopped into the shallow tier and curled up to

69

sleep. "Well, good night," he said.

"Good night," said Fatima. She crossed the courtyard again, blew out her candle, and climbed back into bed. Within seconds, she was sound asleep.

The Thieves

A FEW HOURS LATER, JUST BEFORE DAYBREAK, Fatima was awakened by loud shouts and splashes coming from the pool. She glanced around the room, but her friends were still asleep. Worried that Jasper had fallen into the water, Fatima threw back the covers and hurried into the courtyard.

It was still dark outside, so Fatima carefully made her way to the edge of the pool.

"Jasper!" she called in a hoarse whisper. "Where are you? Are you okay?"

"Watch out!" yelped Jasper. "Thieves! Run!"

But it was too late. Fatima heard footsteps behind her. Before she could scream, a large hand closed over her mouth. Fatima used all her strength to elbow the thief in the stomach. "Oof!" he cried out, but he didn't loosen his hold.

Another man raced toward them from across the courtyard. He was holding a cloth sack filled with huge, rectangular objects. Fatima gasped. From the shapes inside, she thought they might be paintings from her parents' art collection!

"You're a numbskull, Emir!" hissed the man with the cloth sack. He was tall and muscular, with a large, bushy mustache. "We weren't going to wake anybody, remember?

And we were supposed to leave the way we came in!"

"Sorry, Yazid," said Emir. He was smaller than his friend, clean shaven and wiry. "I got lost."

"No kidding," snorted Yazid. "But did you have to fall into the pool?"

"It was an accident!" protested Emir.

"You have too many accidents," said Yazid. "What are we going to do about her?"

Suddenly Jasper piped up. "Unhand her, you villains!"

Startled, Yazid dropped the bag and whirled around, looking in all directions. "Who said that?" he hissed.

Fatima's heart leaped into her throat. She feared what the thieves might do to Jasper if they found him.

"I am an all-powerful genie," Jasper said. "If you do not release Princess Fatima at

once, I will cause a gigantic windstorm to sweep you up and carry you off to prison—where you belong!"

Yazid stroked his mustache. "Really? Well, if you're so all-powerful, how come we can't

even see you?"

"I'm . . . um . . . INVISIBLE!" Jasper
shouted.

Yazid scanned the courtyard, his ears perked.
Suddenly he splashed into the pool and reached

to the top of the fountain. Jasper screamed.

"Gotcha!" said Yazid. Straightening, he squinted at the tiny figure caught in his fist. "Mighty small for a genie, aren't you?"

"Size means nothing," Jasper said bravely. "You'd better put me down, or else I'll . . ."

Yazid laughed. "Or else you'll *what*? If you had any real powers, you would've used them by now." He squeezed Jasper. "I've half a mind to squash you like a bug!"

Jasper gave a frightened yelp.

Fatima moaned. Why couldn't he have just kept quiet?

"On second thought," said Yazid, "I think I'll keep you for a while. You might just know some things that could prove useful." He shoved Jasper into his pocket.

"Let him go!" Fatima screamed. But her words were muffled by Emir's hand.

Emir tightened his grip on her. "What about the princess? Should we tie her up and leave her?"

Yazid nodded. "There's got to be some rope around here somewhere."

But Fatima wasn't about to be tied up. She worked her jaws open, then bit down hard on one of Emir's fingers.

"Yow!" he cried, dropping his hand. As soon as he did, Fatima wriggled out of his grasp and ran.

Emir and Yazid raced after her, but Fatima got away. Rounding a corner, she ducked into her father's study and ran through another door that led to the front of the palace. Gasping for breath, she sank to the ground and thought about what to do next.

The thieves were sure to leave quickly once they realized they'd lost her. Then

Fatima could sneak back into the palace and wake her friends. They'd hop onto her flying carpet, follow the thieves, and plot how to rescue Jasper.

The sound of pounding footsteps cut into Fatima's thoughts. Emir and Yazid were coming!

A short distance away, Fatima spied an old wooden cart half hidden in some bushes. She supposed a gardener had left it there. Inside was an old blanket. Without a moment's pause, Fatima dove into the cart and threw the blanket over herself.

The next thing she knew, something heavy settled on top of her. "Good thing I spotted this cart earlier," said Yazid. "It'll make our getaway faster."

Fatima could barely keep herself from crying out. The bag of paintings was squashing her!

"You push," Yazid said to Emir.

"Why me?" Emir grumbled.

"Because I said so," said Yazid. "And hurry up. As soon as that princess blabs, half of the palace will be after us!"

In a moment the cart began to roll, bumping over the rocky ground. Fortunately, Fatima was able to push the heavy cloth bag to one side to take some of the weight off herself.

Emir grunted and groaned. "These paintings sure are heavy."

"Stop complaining," said Yazid. "Just think of all the money we'll make when we sell them."

Even though she was scared, Fatima stayed hidden. And she listened carefully to figure out where they were going. After a long while, she heard vendors in the distance setting up for the day's bazaar. Stalls were being nailed together. Hammers pounded and chickens squawked. The smell of fried foods and coffee reached Fatima's keen nose. But then the cart veered to the right, away from town.

As the cart rolled along and the noises around her faded, Fatima thought about Jasper. He hadn't uttered a peep since Yazid had dropped him into his pocket. What if Yazid had squashed Jasper, as he'd threatened? Fatima shuddered. She didn't want him to be hurt—or, even worse, *killed*. And what if the thieves discovered her when they unloaded the cart? Blinking back tears, Fatima wondered if she'd ever see Jasper or her family and friends again.

It seemed like forever before the cart finally turned left and jolted to a halt. "Bring the paintings," Yazid barked at Emir.

Fatima froze as the bag was lifted out of the cart. When the thieves walked away, she sighed with relief.

But then she heard Yazid say, "Wait a second." She held her breath as his footsteps came closer. Suddenly the blanket was whipped away. "Hello, Princess," said Yazid. "Did you know your toes were sticking out?"

Locked Up

Fatima gulped. "Thanks for the ride. I think I'll just head home now."

But Yazid stopped her from scrambling out of the cart. He turned to Emir. "It seems we have an unwanted guest."

The thieves escorted Fatima into a ramshackle house. Then Yazid marched her up several flights of stairs and into a small, bare room without any windows. "Sorry for the poor accommodations," he said grimly. "I didn't expect to be hosting royalty." He started to leave.

Fatima's eyes flashed with anger. "Bats and bullfrogs! You can't just keep me here, you know."

Yazid stared at her coldly. "You haven't left me much choice."

She tried to rush past him, but he slipped out of the room and slammed the door in her face. Fatima heard a key turn in the lock and then footsteps clatter down the stairs. She beat on the door with her fists, but it was no use: Yazid did not return.

At last Fatima groped her way to a corner of the dark room and slumped against the wall. Her parents and friends would be up by now. They'd be worried sick when they discovered she was missing. Would they notice Jasper was missing too?

Probably not, Fatima thought sadly. Her friends thought the little genie was still in his bottle. They might think he was just being sulky if they called to him and he didn't come out. And her parents didn't know anything about him. They were bound to notice the missing paintings though, but would they connect them to her disappearance?

Fatima shivered and tucked her nightgown around her bare feet. Her stomach growled. She hadn't had anything to eat since dinner last night. What if Yazid and Emir forgot to feed her? A tear rolled down Fatima's cheek. She'd never felt so helpless before. Had Jasper felt that way too, when he lost all his powers and became small? If only he were with her, at least then she wouldn't feel so lonely.

Wrapping her arms around her knees,

Fatima rocked back and forth as tears gave way to sobs. She was crying so hard, she didn't hear the sound of something being dragged across the floor. She was rocking so hard, she didn't feel something scamper over her foot and climb to her shoulder. But then she heard a soft voice in her ear: "*Shhh*. It'll be okay."

At first Fatima thought that she'd made up the voice to calm herself. But then she heard it again, a whisper: "Hey, Fatima, it's me. Jasper."

He slid down Fatima's shoulder, landing on top of her hand. She brought him closer so she could see him better. "You don't know how glad I am to see you!" she cried. "I was worried you'd been crushed inside Yazid's pocket. How did you escape?"

"Yazid had a hole in his pocket. When I realized he'd locked you in this room, I slid down his pant leg. Then I had to climb back

up the steps and crawl under the door."

"You must be exhausted," Fatima said.

"I am," said Jasper, "but I can't rest now. We've got to get out of here!"

Fatima shook her head sadly. "It's hopeless. The door is locked and . . ."

"Yes, I know," Jasper interrupted. "But I've

got the key."

"What?" exclaimed Fatima. "How?"

"After Yazid locked the door, he dropped it in his pocket," said Jasper. "It landed on my head! I took it with me when I slid through the hole. I left it just over there, against the door."

Fatima would've hugged him if he hadn't

been so small. "Jasper, you're brilliant!"

"Thanks." Jasper was quiet for a moment. Then he said, "I really am sorry I ruined your carpet."

"Don't worry," said Fatima. "You didn't ruin it. It'll still fly, and the broken threads can be mended." She paused. "Anyway, I'm sorry too. I said a lot of mean things to you."

"It's okay," said Jasper. "I didn't blame you for being angry."

Suddenly, loud voices interrupted them. Yazid and Emir were arguing downstairs. "Fifty-fifty!" shouted Emir. "That's what we've always agreed on. Why should you get more than me?"

"Because it was *my* idea," snarled Yazid.

"But I helped!" whined Emir. "I even pushed the cart."

"So?" Yazid said. "You're lucky I'm even giving you twenty percent. Now go to the bazaar and buy some food while I see about finding someone to buy these paintings."

"What about the princess?" asked Emir. "We shouldn't leave her here alone, should we?"

"She's locked up, you lunkhead!" said Yazid. "Even if she screamed her head off, no one would hear. She hasn't got a window to climb out of, and there aren't any houses within a mile of this place."

"They seem to have forgotten all about *you*," Fatima whispered to Jasper.

"People do that when you're as small as I am," the genie said. "But as soon as they leave, we're leaving too. I don't want to be here when Yazid discovers his key is missing. He might remember me then . . . and put two and two together."

Fatima shuddered. Yazid had already threatened to squash Jasper once. And now she was in danger too. She knew far too much for Yazid to let her go.

The two captives held their breaths until the door downstairs slammed shut. After waiting a few minutes longer to make sure neither man returned, Fatima placed Jasper on her shoulder and felt her way along the wall until she reached the door.

"The key is to the right," said Jasper.

Fatima found it and unlocked the door. Then she and Jasper made their escape down the stairs and out of the house. When they reached the road, Fatima looked around carefully, trying to get her bearings. She remembered turning left before the cart had jolted to a stop. They'd need to reverse directions to go back. "We should go right," she said, peering down the road.

She was glad no one was around to see

her. Walking along barefoot didn't bother her—she often did that—but it did feel strange to be outside in her nightgown.

Fatima and Jasper had almost reached the road that would lead them home when they saw someone coming toward them. Fatima froze. It was Emir!

"Run!" Jasper screamed.

Catching sight of Fatima, Emir gave a shout. He dropped his packages from the bazaar and raced after her.

Fatima took off in a zigzag course through an olive grove. She was a fast runner, but no match for Emir. Besides, it was hard to run barefoot and in a nightgown.

Emir was practically on Fatima's heels when her gown caught on a fallen tree branch and she tumbled to the ground.

"Got you!" yelled Emir, making a grab for her leg.

To the Rescue

"OH NO YOU DON'T!" SHOUTED A FAMILIAR voice. It was Tansy! Fatima raised her head just as her three friends swooped down on her flying carpet. Emir drew back, startled, giving Fatima just enough time to leap onto the carpet while Jasper clung to her nightgown.

Lysandra pulled back on the carpet and it rose swiftly into the air. Fatima breathed a

huge sigh of relief and grinned at the others.
"That was *so* close. Thanks for coming to our
rescue!"

Emir jumped up and down and shook his
fist in the air. "Come back!" he yelled.

Fatima waved to him as the carpet sailed

away. "'Bye!" She glanced at Jasper. "You all right?"

"I will be as soon as we land," he said shakily.

"How did you find us?" Fatima asked her friends as they sped back to the palace.

"When we woke and found you missing, we went to ask your parents if they knew where you'd gone," Elena explained. "They'd just discovered some of their paintings were missing too. Then a servant reported seeing two men sneaking away from the palace in the wee hours of the morning. Of course, the servant hadn't suspected the men were thieves."

"When we couldn't find you anywhere inside the palace," said Tansy, "your father went out with a search party. He thought you might have discovered the thieves and been taken hostage."

"They woke me up," said Fatima. "They took Jasper, but I was only captured by accident."

Lysandra nodded. "We thought maybe he was with you when we discovered he wasn't inside his bottle. You don't mind that we borrowed your flying carpet, do you?"

"*Mind?* You've got to be kidding!" Fatima shuddered. "I don't want to think what might've happened if you hadn't come along when you did. But how did you know where to find us?"

"It was Elena's idea," said Tansy. "She wondered if a villager might've seen or heard something suspicious, so we flew over the bazaar. I played my flute so we could hear everyone's thoughts. The man who chased you was there. We heard him thinking about a princess who was locked up in a house." She paused, grinning. "He was wondering what princesses ate, and if you might like bread and cheese."

Fatima smiled. Of the two thieves, Emir was *definitely* more human than Yazid.

"When the man left the bazaar, we hid

behind the tents and watched where he went," added Elena. "We followed at a safe distance. Then we spotted you. When the man started chasing you, we flew in as fast as we could."

"His name's Emir," said Fatima. "His partner, Yazid, said he was going to find someone to buy the paintings they stole from the palace." She paused. "Which way did my father's search party go?"

"Toward those hills," said Lysandra, pointing west. "Do you want to find him before we return to the palace?"

Fatima nodded. As the princesses neared the hills, they spotted King Mustafa at the head of the search party, riding a large, white stallion. They zoomed down to him.

"Fatima!" exclaimed King Mustafa. "You're all right! But what—"

"No time for questions now," interrupted

Fatima. She quickly described the two thieves and told her father how to find the house where she and the paintings had been taken.

King Mustafa sent half of his men to capture the thieves and retrieve the paintings. Then he and the rest of the search party accompanied the princesses back to the palace. Fatima rode with her father on his horse so she could tell him the whole story. Jasper held on tight to her nightgown, bouncing up and down as the horse galloped along. "Not much better than a flying carpet," he muttered.

Fatima introduced Jasper to her father, explaining that he'd lost his genie powers. "But that didn't stop him from rescuing me," she said proudly. Then she told how Jasper had slipped out of Yazid's pocket and dragged the key up to the room where she'd been imprisoned.

Turning in his saddle, King Mustafa bowed to the little genie. "You saved my daughter," he said. "I am forever in your debt."

"I didn't really do much," Jasper said modestly, "but I was glad to help."

"Tonight we will have a big celebration!" King Mustafa declared. Then he growled. "But first we must capture those thieves!"

Celebration

As soon as the princesses arrived back at the palace, Queen Saruca ran to hug Fatima. "Thank goodness you're home. We were so worried about you!"

Fatima told the story of her capture and escape all over again, praising Jasper. "He was *so* brave. He really took a chance, stealing that key. If he'd been caught, Yazid would have squashed him!"

"I was so worried about Fatima, I didn't even think about that," said Jasper. "I sure hope you catch Yazid!"

King Mustafa scowled. "Don't worry. My men will nab him faster than a frog can snap up a fly."

"I can't thank you enough for saving my daughter," Queen Saruca told Jasper. "You may be small and lack magical powers, but you make up for it in cleverness and courage."

Jasper blushed. "You're very kind. But we might have been captured *again* if the other princesses hadn't arrived when they did."

"Jasper's right," said Fatima. "You should see Lysandra fly my carpet. She's a natural. And it was Elena's idea to fly over the bazaar, where Tansy played her flute to listen in on everyone's thoughts. That's how they found Emir."

Queen Saruca smiled at the princesses. "Thank you all," she said. "Fatima is blessed to have such brave and intelligent friends."

Fatima nodded. It was only by combining their princess powers that her friends were able to rescue her. They'd used teamwork! It was lucky for her that Lysandra could fly so well. Fatima decided that if Lysandra ever found a genuine flying carpet to buy, she would try not to be jealous. After all, then they'd have *two* carpets to travel on. And, in the meantime, maybe she'd offer to teach Lysandra how to do loop-the-loops.

As the Banquet Hall was being readied for the promised celebration, the second half of the search party returned, herding Emir and Yazid ahead of them. The thieves were brought before King Mustafa and Queen Saruca in the Throne Room. As soon as he saw Fatima's parents, Yazid dropped to the floor and crawled toward them, begging. "Please, Your Royal Highnesses. Have pity on me. I am not a bad man. Stealing the paintings was Emir's idea. He *made* me do it."

"Why, you . . . ," spluttered Emir. "Don't believe him, Your Majesties! He's lying!"

The two men began to scuffle, but the palace guards pulled them apart. King Mustafa waved his hand for silence. "It seems to me you were equally involved with stealing the paintings, not to mention my daughter's imprisonment!"

Emir slumped to the floor. "It's not fair. It's just not fair!"

"Oh, shut up," growled Yazid.

King Mustafa spoke to the guards. "Take them away."

Yazid snarled at Fatima as the guards led him past, but Emir hung his head. "Sorry, Princess," he mumbled.

Fatima couldn't help pitying him. After all, Emir hadn't been nearly as horrid to her as Yazid. He'd even been worried about what she might like to eat. She'd urge her father to make Emir's sentence a lighter one.

The celebration began after dinner. There were performances by acrobats and jugglers, followed by singing and dancing. The princesses took turns letting Jasper perch on their shoulders so he wouldn't get trampled on the ballroom floor.

Toward the end of the evening, King Mustafa stood at the front of the room and clapped for everyone's attention. When the room quieted, he said, "Tonight we celebrate the return of my daughter, Princess

Fatima. I now would like to publicly thank everyone who played a part in her rescue— or in the capture of the scoundrels who held her hostage."

One by one, King Mustafa called up the members of the search party, the three princesses, and Jasper. He shook the men's hands, and kissed Lysandra, Tansy, and Elena on the cheek. Then he bent down to Jasper, who climbed onto the king's hand. Raising him high above his head, King Mustafa declared, "Though small in size, and stripped of his powers, this little genie risked his life to bring my daughter the key that set her free. Let us all acknowledge his heroism."

"Hooray for the little genie!" a servant shouted. Then everyone began to chant: "Jasper! Jasper! Jasper!"

Suddenly a golden light began to glow

around him. Everyone oohed and aahed in amazement as it shone brighter and brighter. Enveloped in a shimmering blaze, Jasper rose up from King Mustafa's hand and began to grow larger. When he was as big around as an elephant—and twice as tall as the king—the light broke into a shower of sparks and disappeared.

"Look at me!" Jasper whooped in a voice as loud as thunder. "I'm myself again!" He stretched one hand up to touch the ceiling and then swooped across the room. "I can fly!" he boomed. Jasper pointed to Fatima's carpet, which was rolled up and leaning against her chair. "Repair it!" he roared. Instantly, the broken threads were mended.

Astonished, Fatima ran her fingers over the carpet. "Your powers are back! My carpet

looks beautiful. Thank you, Jasper!"

He beamed. "You're welcome, my friend."

When the celebration was over, the princesses and Jasper retired to Fatima's quar-

ters. "I don't understand why your powers didn't come back when you brought Fatima the key," said Tansy. "Why didn't it happen until the celebration?"

Elena smiled. "I think I know. The Grand Genie said Jasper's powers would return 'on the day everyone acknowledged he no longer needed them.' And that's what happened when King Mustafa praised Jasper and we all cheered."

"Now that you're yourself again, what will you do?" asked Lysandra.

"I'll grant wishes, of course," said Jasper.

"But I set you free," said Fatima. "You're your own master now, remember?"

"I know," said Jasper. "But I still want to help others. Only from now on I'll try not to show off. I'll give just the amount of help people really need."

"Will you be leaving soon?" asked Fatima sadly.

Jasper nodded. "I'll leave tonight. Like you told me, the world's a big place and there's a lot to see."

"I suppose I did say that," said Fatima. A lump formed in her throat. "But I'll miss you." Noticing the glum looks on her friends' faces, she quickly added, "We'll *all* miss you."

"And I'll miss all of *you*," said Jasper. "But don't worry. I'll come back to visit. I'll want to share my adventures—and hear about yours, too."

"Speaking of adventures," said Lysandra, "*this* has been one I'll never forget."

"Me neither," said Tansy.

"We certainly do have exciting times together," Elena said.

"That's for sure," Fatima agreed. "I can't say I enjoyed every single part of this adventure, but what matters most is getting to the happy ending."

"Exactly," said Tansy.

"I'm hungry," Lysandra said suddenly. She glanced at Fatima's tree and licked her lips. "I wish I had one of those oranges."

"Me too!" everyone else exclaimed.

Jasper smiled. "Granted." He waved an arm
and four beautiful oranges floated into the
princesses' waiting hands.

BOCA RATON PUBLIC LIBRARY, FLORIDA

3 3656 0461659 8

Check out all the Princess Power adventures!

Princess Power #1: The Perfectly Proper Prince

Princess Lysandra wants adventure! So when she meets Fatima, Elena, and Tansy, she couldn't be happier. But their first quest comes even sooner than expected, when they stumble upon a frog that just *might* have royal blood!

Princess Power #2: The Charmingly Clever Cousin

Princess Fatima doesn't like her brother-in-law, Ahmed, as much as his cousin Yusuf. Yet when Ahmed goes missing, Fatima starts to worry. And it just might be up to the princesses to rescue him!

J
Williams, Suzanne,
The gigantic, genuine
 genie /

...ry Ogre

...rbidden to fight ...to try. Can Tansy ...e?

Princess Po...

Princess Elena finds a beautiful comb that softens her frizzy hair. However, she starts dreaming of a green-haired maiden who cries that she can't live without her comb. Will the princesses be able to find the maiden before it's too late?

Princess Power #5: The Stubbornly Secretive Servant

The princesses are having a ball visiting Lysandra's sister, Gabriella. And they can't wait for handsome Prince Jonathon to join them. But when he never arrives, everyone panics. They must find the missing prince *without* the help of his stubborn servant.

Princess Power #6: The Gigantic, Genuine Genie

Princess Fatima buys a beautiful bottle that supposedly holds a real genie. But it turns out that the genie is tiny and powerless! Will the princesses be able to restore his size and magical touch?

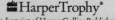 **HarperTrophy**®
An Imprint of HarperCollinsPublishers

www.harpercollinschildrens.com